For you to read:

In our engaging tale, two children are challenged by a mountain landslide, and they encounter a bear. Please see an article at the end of the story to learn about landslides in New England, like the one pictured here that rumbled down Mount Moosilauke in New Hampshire during Tropical Storm Irene in 2011.

Please see a second article in the back about New England's black bears. It explains the behavior of the young bear that Gina and Harold confront in our story.

Thank you to:

• Kathie Aldrich Côté, owner of Polly's Pancake Parlor, Sugar Hill, New Hampshire,
for suggesting a children's story about camping from Free People Publishing.

• Daniel Bailey, Bear Project Leader and Wildlife Damage Biologist for the New Hampshire Fish and Game Department,
for teaching our writer about New England black bears.

• Steve Smith, owner of The Mountain Wanderer Map and Book Store in Lincoln, New Hampshire,
for in-depth information about landslides in New England, and the upper photo here.

• Thom Davis, Professor Emeritus of Natural and Applied Sciences, Bentley University in Waltham, Massachusetts,
for writing our landslide article.

• Daniel Berna, wildlife photographer who is based in Vermont,
for the bear photo here and on the last page; see danielberna.com.

Lessons from our changing Earth

The mountain landslide that challenges Harold and Gina in our story is an example of how landforms constantly remake themselves. We scarcely notice, because the Earth works on a timescale that is much, much longer than human lifespans. Our story also teaches children about reaching maturity according to Nature's lifecycle, when they witness a bear sent off to begin its adult life.

Gina camped with her mother in a tent, at a campground in the forest beside a wide and bouncing brook. Harold camped with his mother and father in a tent near Gina's.

A Bear in Camp with Harold and Gina

To learn more about illustrator Daniel Pantano and writer Jeffrey Zygmont, go to the People page at freepeepub.com.

A Bear in Camp with Harold and Gina

Free People Publishing
Salem, NH
freepeepub.com

ISBN: 978-1-959341-05-5
Library of Congress Control Number: 2025931160

Printed in the United States of America

During the first night, Gina woke when she heard very loud growling and rowling, grumbling and rumbling and wailing and moaning near their campsite. Gina felt frightened. She snuggled deeply down into her sleeping bag to hide.

In the morning she told her mom about the loud sounds.

"I was so tired that I didn't wake up," answered Gina's mom.

When Gina told Harold, he said the noise must have come from a ghost, or a monster.

TAP
TAP
GROWL
RUSTLE

The second night, Gina heard the rowling and wailing and very loud moaning again. Next she heard rustling and shuffling and scratching and footsteps near the tent. A ghost? A monster? No, Gina decided, Harold is wrong. Very quietly she crawled from her sleeping bag. Very quietly she opened the zipper of the tent door. Poking her head through the opening, Gina saw a bear.

She felt very frightened, and scrunched deeply down into her sleeping bag once more.

In the morning she told her mother.

"It's looking for food," Gina's mom explained. "But everyone camping here keeps their food sealed away. And we clean up our garbage carefully. But bears are powerful animals with sharp teeth and claws. If you see it again, tell me and we'll all yell and clap and bang on pots to scare it away."

When Gina heard the bear in the campsite early on the third morning, she woke her mother, who shouted to the other campers, who all together rose out of their tents and shouted loudly and clapped their hands and banged on campfire cooking pots. The clamorous racket scared the bear. It scurried away quickly, splashing across the brook and disappearing into the woods beyond.

After breakfast, Harold and Gina asked if they could walk together on a trail that led to a pretty waterfall nearby.

"Come back right away," said Gina's mom. "We'll have the campsite cleaned up by then and we can all go on a long hike together."

"And make sure you stay on the trail," added Harold's dad. "It's easy to get confused and get lost if you go off the trail and into the woods."

The children hopped on stones to cross the gurgling brook. The trail led them around a steep slope and beside a lofty stone cliff towering above them.

When they had almost reached the waterfall, Gina stopped suddenly.

"Look. That pesky bear is just ahead of us," she said.

"Oh, what's he doing here?" groaned Harold.

Suddenly an enormous crack and crash
and rumble roared from behind them.
The terrified children ran away
from the thundering noise.
The bear ran away
from it too.

The three stood together, looking back at what had just been a very big landslide. Loosened by time and weather, a large section of stone had broken free from the cliff behind Harold and Gina. As it fell it pulled down other big sections of rock and tore up soil and uprooted trees. The huge fallen jumble of broken stone and shattered trees and churned up dirt now lay in a rough, wide barrier that covered the trail back to the camp.

When Harold noticed the bear beside them, he said, "Hey, this bear isn't bad. This bear is sad."

Gina jumped back from the bear in surprise. But before she could do more, the gloomy bear said, "You'd be sad too if your mother chased you away."

"What?" Harold wondered. "Mothers don't do that."

"Mine did," said the bear. "She said I couldn't stay with her anymore."

"But why?" Gina joined in.

"She said it's Nature's way," answered the bear. "After I was born I was with her for two winters. But now she says I'm big enough to live on my own. I feel so alone that all I do is cry."

"That's what woke me at our campsite," Gina exclaimed.

Harold looked at the huge heap of rubble from the landslide. "How will we get back to camp now?" he wondered. "The trail is buried under that big mess of rocks."

The glum bear said, "If I had a place to go back to, I'd walk through the woods to find the trail on the other side of that messy landslide."

"But we'll get lost in the woods," Gina worried. "Without a path to follow, we'll turn the wrong way."

"Oh, just follow me," grumped the bear. "I've been through there a hundred times. I'll take you."

Harold and Gina stayed close behind as the bear padded among the trees.

But deep inside the forest, the bear stopped where clusters of shiny round berries grew on the branches of low hobblebush shrubs. The bear sat. The bear pulled berry clusters into its mouth and chewed slowly.

"Ummm," it murmured gratefully. "My mom showed me these berries last summer. They're delicious."

"Our parents must be worried by now," Gina said. She scolded the bear, "Can you stop eating for a while and show us the way back to the trail?"

"Look at how big I am," it answered. "Bears need a lot of food. Bears spend a lot of time eating."

Gina and Harold peered at the forest all around them. Tall trunks of trees loomed everywhere. Smaller, younger trees stretched up among them. Low-growing shrubs and ground plants spread under the shadows on the rough forest floor.

"We'll never find our way out of here," marveled Harold.

Through the trees, another bear appeared. It stopped to eat berries where other hobblebush plants grew.

"Now that's interesting," said the bear with Harold and Gina. "I'll go closer to find out what that new bear is like."

"But what about our trail?" Gina yelled to the animal as it slowly loped away.

"We'll never find it by ourselves," Harold said.

The two children huddled together closely beneath the dark, silent trees.

Suddenly they heard crashing footfalls rushing toward them. Harold's parents and Gina's mom came running. Harold's dad held a map and compass to help guide them.

"Thank goodness you're safe," exclaimed Gina's mother.

"When we heard the rock slide we came right away," Harold's mom explained.

"Oh, we were fine," boasted Harold. "That bear from our camp was showing us the way back."

The adults looked at Harold and wondered.

"Now is not the time for stories," said his dad.

"We're just glad we found you
both safe and sound,"
said his mom.

Gina wondered what to tell them about the bear. She said, "That bear in our camp was hungry and lonely because its mother had chased it away."

"She was mean," added Harold.

"No. That's Nature's way," explained Gina's mom. "After two winters, the bear is big enough to be on its own, and the mother is ready to have a new baby, a new bear cub. That's Nature's way of making sure there are always more bears."

"And we're happy that we'll always have more of you two," beamed Harold's mother.

"My compass will show us the direction to take back to camp," Harold's father said. "Let's head back and get ready for that long hike we talked about."

"But this time let's stay far away from rock slides," said Harold.

THE END

Landslides Show Earth Re-Shaping Itself

The landslide in our story is a dramatic event that reshapes a mountain. The physical forces and conditions that caused it, and more, are explained below by **P. Thompson Davis, Professor Emeritus, Geology and Paleoclimatology, Bentley University, Waltham, Massachusetts.**

The word *landslide* is a generic term that covers a wide range of landform changes and processes that shape Earth's surface by the downward movement of soil and rock. Gravity is a primary driving force. The main type of landslide in the New England region, encompassing the White Mountains of New Hampshire, Katahdin in Maine, the Adirondacks in upper New York, and others, is called a *debris flow*. It is a rapid mass movement almost always triggered by unusually heavy rain.

Humans rarely witness debris-flow types of landslides because they occur on remote mountainous terrain and in weather that is usually too intolerable for people. However, during extremely wet storms like the Great New England Hurricane of 1938, Tropical Storm Irene in late August 2011, and the unnamed Halloween storm in 2017, fresh debris flows are often widely found.

"There can be years without any. Then you can have one storm that causes a dozen," explains Steve Smith, who operates The Mountain Wanderer Book and Map Store in Lincoln, New Hampshire, an information center for hikers. Steve is also editor of the Appalachian Mountain Club's *White Mountain Guide.* He has visited nearly all of the debris-flow sites in the White Mountains, many of them several times. I have visited several of the more remote sites with him, typically involving long approaches, extensive off-trail bushwhacking, and descents after nightfall. Since 2009 Steve has documented his backcountry excursions – with extensive photographs – in a blog. And over the past decade he has compiled *Landslides of the White Mountains*, a very comprehensive online document. Both are available through his store's website, mountainwanderer.com.

Landslides are categorized primarily by their speed of movement, types of materials, and the amount of water involved. The fastest mass movements, called rock falls and topples, involve free falling, bouncing, and rolling blocks. Topples also include rotation, like a diver from a high board. In June 1977, a rock fall from Cannon Cliff in Franconia Notch of the White Mountains deposited a large, angular block of bedrock at the bottom on Cannon's talus slope. *Talus* is the term for the thousands of such blocks that have been falling and accumulating at the base of the cliff since the last ice sheet covering North America receded over 12,000 years ago. You can see 1977's large, long-traveling block from the paved bike path south of the notch's Profile Lake. Another, more famous rock fall/topple from Cannon was the loss of New Hampshire's iconic Old Man of the Mountain rock formation on May 5, 2003.

Rather than heavy rainfall, mechanical and chemical weathering caused those two falls. Mechanical weathering involves frost expanding in cracks, splitting solid bedrock into separate blocks. Chemical weathering is the decay of minerals in bedrock veins and seams, creating separations.

Slower, but still very rapid mass movements include debris and rock avalanches, earth flows, and the debris flows already mentioned. Earth flows and debris flows are influenced by absorbed water that increases *pore water pressure*. It forces soil particles apart from one another, making them more mobile and susceptible to gravity's pull.

A classic example of a fast-moving rock avalanche occurred in early September 2022 on Eagle Cliff, across from the Cannon Tramway in Franconia Notch. It is still clearly visible because new vegetation has not yet grown enough to heal the avalanche scar. Also in Franconia Notch, both north and south of Profile Lake, landslide scars on the ridge along the west flank of Mount Lafayette are becoming less visible because of re-vegetation.

In 1947 and 1959, heavy rains caused massive debris flows along the many slide paths there, which buried and closed old Route 3 (now Interstate Route 93) under masses of rock and sediment that took several days to clear. Fine-grained sediments from those debris flows were deposited in Profile Lake. When geologists retrieved sediment cores from the lake, they learned that debris flows of similar magnitude have occurred for more than 12,000 years, since de-glaciation of the White Mountains.

Thus Franconia Notch is a good place to view several landslide features that are less remote than the slide encountered by the campers in this story.

A Bear's Journey through Noble Nature

The orphaned bear at the start of our story has not been poorly treated by its mother. Both mother bear and cub are faithfully performing the noble roles that Nature assigns.

The distressed cub that is crying in the campsite has grown to be a yearling. It is eighteen months old. It has spent two winters sleeping alongside its mother in a sheltered den, and through its first year and a half of life, its mom has taught the young bear the skills it needs to survive.

Its most important skill is finding food. Our northeastern black bears are omnivores that eat a wide variety of foods. For meat, a bear might kill a fawn, backyard poultry, or even young livestock on farms. But primarily it follows the seasons and forages for plants.

That starts when snow melt and warming temperatures wake a bear from its winter sleep in March or April. Emerging from its den and eager to eat, the bear first seeks fresh grasses, leafy plants like dandelions, and emerging leaves on shrubs and trees. Its food is meager until wild blueberries, strawberries, and other small fruits ripen in early July. Larger fruits like apples and cherries come next. Finally, the crop of wild nuts like acorns and beechnuts allows the bear to fully fatten before winter arrives. By the time cold weather and snow make food impossible to find, the bear is in its best nourished, best physical condition for its long torpor, or semi-hibernating sleep.

That's when female bears, called sows, give birth. In January every two years, a sow bears a litter averaging two or three cubs. The baby bears weigh just one pound at birth. They nurse in their den through the remainder of Winter. By the time they emerge with their mother in Spring, the cubs have grown six to eight times their birth size, weighing six to eight pounds. That's a little larger than a wild rabbit.

Once in the open, the cubs wean very quickly from their mother's milk. The sow begins educating her cubs about where and when to find specific foods, following the seasonal pattern we just described. Feeding is learned behavior for bears, and mothers are the teachers.

After their schooling through one full seasonal cycle, from grasses and leafy plants to larger fruits, to nutrition-packed nuts, the cubs retire with the sow to sleep through Winter. Their den is a sheltered and secluded cavity, like the hollow beneath the roots of a toppled tree, or a crevice deep under overhanging rocks.

When the bears emerge together again the following Spring, the cubs have grown to be yearlings, the designation given to eighteen- to twenty-four-month-old bears Fully educated by the sow the prior year, the young bears now are well prepared to live independently. The sow drives them away. She has to, because her body is prepared to mate again with a male, and so continue Nature's noble cycle of regeneration, or life-sustaining re-population.

A sow mates with a male bear, called a boar, at the start of summer, in late June or early July. The following January, inside a protective den, she gives the world a new litter of one-pound nursing cubs.

Bears can live into their thirties, repeating that two-year breeding cycle.

The yearlings that she drove away the prior spring, just before the sow and boar mated, raised an enormous racket when they first were orphaned. Those were the protests that Gina hears from the young bear at the start of our story. But they adapt comfortably to independence and soon wander off to establish their own territories. Fully mature in their third or fourth year of life, these new sows and boars mate themselves, bringing the world more marvelous bears.